Magical stories for 5 year Olds

Helen Paiba was one of the most committed, knowledgeable and acclaimed children's booksellers in Britain. For more than twenty years she owned and ran the Children's Bookshop in Muswell Hill, London, which under her guidance gained a superb reputation for its range of children's books and for the advice available to its customers.

Helen was also involved with the Booksellers Association for many years and served on both its Children's Bookselling Group and the Trade Practices Committee.

In 1995 she was given honorary life membership of the Booksellers Association of Great Britain and Ireland in recognition of her outstanding services to the association and to the book trade. In the same year the Children's Book Circle (sponsored by Books for Children) honoured her with the Eleanor Farjeon Award, given for distinguished service to the world of children's books.

Books in this series

Funny Stories for 5 Year Olds

Funny Stories for 6 Year Olds

Funny Stories for 7 Year Olds

Funny Stories for 8 Year Olds

Magical Stories for 5 Year Olds

Magical Stories for 6 Year Olds

Scary Stories for 7 Year Olds

Magical stories for 5 year Olds

Chosen by Helen Paiba

Illustrated by Anthony Lewis

MACMILLAN CHILDREN'S BOOKS

First published 2000 by Macmillan Children's Books

This edition published 2016 by Macmillan Children's Books
an imprint of Pan Macmillan
20 New Wharf Road, London N1 9RR
Associated companies throughout the world
www.panmacmillan.com

ISBN 978-1-5098-0617-1

1 3 5 7 9 8 6 4 2

A CIP catalogue record for this book is available from
the British Library.

Typeset by SX Composing DTP, Rayleigh, Essex
Printed and bound by CPI Group (UK) Ltd, Croydon CR0 4YY

Contents

The Cow Who Flew

Andrew Matthews

Most of you will have heard the story of Jack, who sold his cow to a strange old man for five magic beans. As you know, the beans grew into a beanstalk that reached right up into the clouds, and when Jack climbed it, he got into a bit of bother with an ogre. But what the story doesn't say, is what happened to Jack's cow – and it's high time the truth was told.

It was like this.

Right from the start, Cow had been suspicious of the strange old man who stopped Jack in a wood and offered him the magic beans. "I think there's something peculiar going on here," Cow said to herself, as the old man led her away. For instead of following the path that went out of the trees and into the sunshine, the old man took the path that wound deeper and deeper into the shadows. The air turned cool, and was filled with the croaking of frogs. Toadstools grew in clumps at the edge of the path and they glowed in the dimness.

"I'm not sure I like the look of this," Cow said to herself.

The further they went into the wood, the stranger the strange old man became. He took off his hat, and Cow saw that his ears were long and pointed. Then he took off his coat, and Cow saw his spindly arms and legs, and his knees that were knobblier than two bags of walnuts.

"Well, if he isn't a wood goblin, I'll eat my horns!" said Cow.

The goblin laughed nastily. "Tee hee!" he cried. "Just think – a cow for five beans! That lad Jack was even more stupid than he looked. Now I'll have milk and cream, and butter and cheese whenever I want!"

"That's what you think!" murmured Cow. "My old Ma told me to keep well clear of goblins."

The goblin lived right in the middle of the wood. He had cleared away some trees and built himself a shack. Next to the shack was a small patch of grass, and next to that were the goblin's beans.

The goblin tethered Cow to a post set in the grass. "There you are," he said. "Eat all the grass you want, but don't touch my beans. My old Ma told me never to mix milk with magic." And he left Cow there, all day and all night.

Now Cow was used to spending the night in a cosy barn. She didn't like being out in the open with just the moon and stars for company, so when the sun rose, Cow was in a humpty, grumpy sort of mood.

The goblin came out of his shack with a three-legged stool, a wooden pail and a grin that showed all his crooked teeth. "Now for some lovely creamy milk!" he gloated.

"That's what you think!" muttered Cow.

The goblin put his pail underneath Cow, sat on the stool

and tried to milk her. He teased and squeezed and tickled and tugged until his whiskers turned blue, but he didn't get a single drop of milk from Cow.

Up sprang the goblin, as angry as a stinging wasp. "That rotten, no-good Jack has swindled me!" he

roared. He fixed Cow with a stare that was sourer than lemon juice. "You've got one more chance!" he said. "You give me plenty of milk this evening, or else!" And with that he stamped his foot so hard that the walls of his shack shook.

"Oh dear!" said Cow. "My old Ma was quite right – goblins are a bad lot!"

All day long, Cow chewed grass and thought milky thoughts, But the grass was poor stuff and dry as old pillows.

At sundown, the goblin came out of his shack with his stool and pail. He teased and squeezed and tickled and tugged until his whiskers turned green, but he didn't get a single drop of milk from Cow, and he flew into a terrible rage. "This is your last chance!" he screeched. "If you don't give me a pailful of milk tomorrow morning, I'm going to slice you into steaks, grind you into mince and boil up the leftovers to make stew!" And he stamped his foot so hard that his shack nearly fell down.

Cow trembled with fear. She didn't like the idea of being sliced, ground and boiled. "Whatever can I do?" she whimpered. "I can't make milk from dry grass! I must eat something green and juicy."

Just then, the moon came up, and its light shone down on the plump, luscious beans in the goblin's garden.

"I've got to eat some!" said Cow. "Magic or not, they're my only chance!"

Cow took the tether in her mouth and pulled until it snapped. Then she walked over to the garden and started to munch as quietly as she could. "My goodness, these beans taste grand!" said Cow. "I think I'll eat them all."

But before she could finish the beans, their magic began to work. Cow felt most peculiar, and her back tingled and itched. She turned her head to try and scratch her back with one of her horns, and mooed in amazement. She had grown a pair of enormous wings, with feathers as white and soft as a snowy owl's.

"Goodness me, whatever next?" said Cow. "I'll just give them a quick shake to see if that stops the itching."

The white wings sighed as they flapped, and Cow felt herself rise into the air. With every wing sigh she rose higher, until the goblin's shack was no more than a dot on the ground far below.

Cow soared and swooped,

laughing out loud. "I haven't had so much fun since I was a calf!" she declared. She flew low so that her hooves brushed the tree tops, then flew high, so she could feel the moonlight glistening on her wings.

But as the night wore on, the

magic of the beans wore off. Slowly, Cow's wings started to shrink, until they were too small to lift her. She landed near a cottage, not far from a hidden valley. Tired out by all her flying, Cow fell asleep and the last of the magic turned into a sweet dream.

When the goblin went out of his shack the next morning and found that Cow had escaped, he lost his temper good and proper. He stamped his foot so hard that the ground cracked open and swallowed him up.

As for Cow, well, of course she had landed near the cottage where Donkey, Cat, Dog and Cockerel lived and they made her so welcome that she decided to stay. She moved into the old dairy in Boggart Hollow, where she remained in comfort for the rest of her days.

And she never had anything to do with goblins ever again.

The Mermaid's Crown

Ruth Ainsworth

Peter and Rose lived in a cottage by the sea. It had a tiny garden, but that did not matter. There were no parks or playgrounds nearby, but that was not important either. The children always played on the beach, summer and winter.

In the summer they scrambled over the rocks and paddled in the pools, and Rose made houses of stones and sand, with gardens of seaweed and shells. They were pretty enough to live in.

In the winter they often played in wellingtons and sometimes had to shelter in a cave or against a rock. But the beach was lovely to play on, all the year round.

They liked to play on a flat rock, jutting out into the sea with a pool on one side.

One winter's day, Rose was fishing bits of seaweed out of the pool to make a garden. The seaweed was cold and slippery and her hands were frozen, but she had nearly enough when, reaching out for a wavy purple ribbon, she saw something floating deep down.

"Peter, come and help. I can see something lovely but I can't reach it. Hold my legs."

Peter held her legs tightly and she rolled up her sleeve and reached into the icy water.

"I've got it – no, it has slipped away – now I've got it again. Hold tight!"

She brought up something neither child had ever seen before. It was a circle of seaweed, not floppy, but firm, and mixed with the weed were shells and shining stones.

"It's like a crown," said Peter.

"And it's mine," said Rose,

putting it on her head. "It's my very own." It fitted perfectly.

Their parents examined it and talked about it, but could not decide how it had got into the pool. Perhaps from a wreck? They thought the pink stones were coral and the yellow ones amber. After a few days of talking and wondering they lost interest.

Rose had only one safe place in the house, a wooden box with a lock which she called her treasure box. She kept the crown in this when she wasn't wearing it.

Christmas was getting near and their father put the tree in the tub in the sitting-room. That afternoon the children began to decorate it. All the decorations from previous years were kept in a big cardboard box. While they were busy, Rose suddenly cried out, "Peter! Someone looked in at the window."

Peter turned round, but there was no one there. Then Rose called out again, "Look! Quickly!" This time Peter saw a face for an instant. Then it disappeared. He opened the window and jumped out and a little later appeared at the door, leading someone by the hand. It was a mermaid, or rather a mermaid child, about Rose's size.

The mermaid had long golden hair, sad grey eyes, a pale face and a fishy tail. At first she looked round the room in silence. Then she turned to Rose and spoke.

"I want my crown back."

"So it was yours," said Rose. "I didn't know whose it was. I found it floating in the pool. No one was bothering about it. It's mine now."

"But I want it."

"So do I," said Rose. "Will you have something off the Christmas tree instead? Something pretty?"

The mermaid liked the tree. She touched the baubles and the candles very gently and stroked the glass bird. She looked up at

the angel who stood at the very top. Then she pointed to a string of tinsel, shining among the dark pine needles.

"Please. For my head."

Rose untwined the tinsel and put it round the mermaid's hair.

"Look in the glass," she said.

The mermaid balanced on a stool and looked at herself in the mirror on the wall.

"It will do," she said gravely and then, quick as a fish leaping, she flashed across the floor, out of the window, and away.

"I shan't tell Mother about the mermaid," said Rose.

They almost forgot about the

mermaid as the weeks went by and they saw no sign of her. Rose thought of her when she wore her crown and when she locked it in her treasure box. At Easter time they got their Easter eggs ready. The village shop only had plain chocolate ones but they wrapped them in coloured paper and tied them up with ribbon that their mother had given them. Suddenly they felt they were being watched. There, outside the window, was the mermaid. Peter let her in.

"I want my crown," she said. "The silver one came to pieces, bit by bit. There's nothing left."

"But I want it too," said Rose,

"and it's mine now. Will you choose a ribbon instead?"

The mermaid looked at the ribbons and touched a red one.

"For my hair, please."

Peter tied the bow as his bows were better than Rose's. Again the mermaid looked at herself in the mirror. Then, quick as a fish leaping, she slipped across the floor and out of the window and away.

Rose hoped she would never come back again, and once more she did not tell her mother what had happened. She did not often wear the crown either, though she looked at it almost every day. The seaweed still shone as if it were wet.

But it was not many weeks before the mermaid appeared a third time. The children were picking kingcups in the stream when she rose, suddenly, from the reeds nearby.

"I want my crown," she said. "The red one kept slipping off and the fishes nibbled it. It isn't pretty any more."

"You should never have let the old one go if you loved it so much," said Rose. "Shall I make you a wreath of kingcups? A golden crown?"

"A golden crown," repeated the mermaid. "Yes," and she almost smiled.

Rose made the crown like a daisy chain, slitting a stalk with her fingernail and drawing the next flower through. The mermaid looked at herself in the water.

"Gold," she whispered. "Better than silver or scarlet."

She flashed through the reeds and grasses and disappeared towards the seashore.

In less than a week she was back, her pale face pressed against the window.

"I must have my crown. The gold one drooped and faded and died. My father is a Lord of the Sea and he is going to a banquet with the other Lords. My mother and I are going too. We must all wear our crowns. So I need mine."

Rose saw two tears on the mermaid's cheeks and this time she did not hesitate.

"You shall have it. I'll fetch it."

She ran upstairs, unlocked her treasure box, and brought the crown down. The mermaid put it on and clapped her hands with joy.

"Come to the flat rock in three days' time," she said, before she flashed through the window. With a twist and a twirl, she was gone.

After three days the children went to the flat rock and there, on a bed of seaweed, was an oyster shell. It was tightly closed. When their father opened it, there was a pearl inside. Rose kept it in her treasure box to be made into a ring for her, when she was older and her fingers had stopped growing.

"That will remind you of the mermaid for ever," said her mother, who now knew the whole story.

"I'll remember her even without a pearl," said Rose. "I'll remember her golden hair and her pale face and her fishy tail, and her lovely crown. I knew it was really hers, not mine."

Mrs Simkin and the Magic Wheelbarrow

Linda Allen

One day Mrs Simkin bought a new wheelbarrow. It was bright yellow with a red wheel and green handles.

Mr Simkin said it was much too pretty to use for carrying the garden rubbish.

"But what else can we use it for?" said Mrs Simkin. She

thought for a moment. "I know! We can use it for riding in."

"Good idea!" said Mr Simkin. "Jump in and I will give you a ride."

So Mrs Simkin jumped into the wheelbarrow and Mr Simkin pushed her around the garden. Then they swapped places. It was great fun.

The lady next door looked over the hedge to see what was happening.

"Why are you sitting in that wheelbarrow?" she asked.

Mrs Simkin told her that she was having a ride.

The lady next door said it was a very silly thing to do.

But Mrs Simkin laughed. “But it’s a magic wheelbarrow,” she said. “The only magic wheelbarrow in the world. When I sit in it I don’t feel like Mrs Simkin any more. I feel like a queen.”

“Magic wheelbarrow indeed! What nonsense!” said the lady next door. And she went away, looking cross.

All day long the wheelbarrow stood in the garden, just like any other wheelbarrow.

Mrs Simkin put pots of flowers in it and Mr Simkin tied ribbons around the handles. It looked very smart.

When it was bedtime Mrs Simkin said, "Let's go outside and say goodnight to the wheelbarrow before we go to bed."

"Good idea," said Mr Simkin.

"It's a beautiful night," said Mr Simkin. "Would you like a ride?"

"Oh yes!" cried Mrs Simkin. "That would be lovely."

She got into the wheelbarrow, and as soon as she sat down

something wonderful happened.

Suddenly Mrs Simkin was sitting in a beautiful boat. Mr Simkin was standing at the back, dressed in a black and silver cloak. On his head he had a large blue hat. He had grown curly whiskers.

Mr Simkin pushed the boat along with a pole and began to sing. Mrs Simkin joined in. She was very happy. They sailed around the garden in the moonlight.

After a while the boat became a wheelbarrow again. Mr and Mrs Simkin went indoors and had some cocoa.

"It really *is* a magic wheelbarrow," said Mrs Simkin as

they went upstairs to bed.

The next morning, Mr Robinson, the milkman, came by.

"A little bird tells me that you have a magic wheelbarrow," he said.

"Quite true," replied Mr Simkin. "Come and look."

Mr Robinson said it was a very nice wheelbarrow, but he did not believe that it was a magic one.

Mr Simkin gave him a ride, but nothing magical happened.

"Try sitting backwards," said Mrs Simkin.

But that didn't work, either.

"I cannot understand it," said Mrs Simkin. "It's a magic wheelbarrow when I sit in it."

"Perhaps you are the one who makes the magic, my dear," said Mr Simkin. "If you sit in the wheelbarrow with Mr Robinson it is sure to work."

But still nothing magical happened.

The lady next door said she had never seen such a thing in her life.

When night-time came again,

Mrs Simkin climbed into the wheelbarrow all by herself.

Suddenly she was sitting upon a magnificent white horse. Mr Simkin was sitting behind her. They galloped round and round the garden.

The lady next door was watching them. She couldn't believe her eyes!

When morning came, she told all the people in the street what she had seen.

Nobody believed her.

"Then come to my house tonight," she said, "and see what happens."

That night the moon was very bright. It was almost as light as day.

Mrs Simkin said, "Our wheelbarrow is sure to turn into something very special tonight, Stanley."

Mr and Mrs Simkin didn't know that all the people were watching over the hedge.

As Mrs Simkin stepped into the wheelbarrow . . . it turned into a magnificent glass coach.

Mrs Simkin had a crown on her head. Mr Simkin had a top hat.

The coach was drawn by six white horses.

The lady next door tried to keep the people quiet, but they were too excited. When Mrs Simkin passed by in her coach they all cheered.

Mrs Simkin bowed to them, and waved like a queen.

The next day all the people who lived in the street went to buy new wheelbarrows.

They waited until it was night-time and then they gave each other rides. Everyone had a lot of fun, but nothing magical happened. The wheelbarrows weren't magic ones, like Mrs Simkin's.

The people were disappointed. They went to Mrs Simkin's house to complain.

"We have all bought wheel-barrows," they said. "They look just like yours, but they won't change into anything special. We have spent our money for nothing."

"We told the lady next door that ours was the only magic wheelbarrow in the world," said Mr Simkin. "You can't blame us."

But the people were so cross that Mrs Simkin said, "Listen. I will buy your wheelbarrows if you don't want them any more. I like to have plenty of wheelbarrows about the place."

She gave the people their money and they left their wheelbarrows in her garden.

That night Mrs Simkin said, "Come out into the garden, Stanley. I want you to do something for me." And she told

Mr Simkin to tie the wheelbarrows together, in a row.

When the moon was high in the sky, Mrs Simkin stepped into the first wheelbarrow.

And then something truly magical happened . . .

"All aboard!" cried Mr Simkin, waving his flag.

The Three Bears

Catherine Storr

Lisa is a little girl who likes to read fairy tales. She thinks she could do better than the heroines of the stories, but when she mysteriously finds herself in Goldilocks' shoes, she finds that things don't turn out quite as she planned.

"I wouldn't have eaten any of the porridge," Lisa said.

"What porridge?"

“The porridge Goldilocks found in the bears’ house. I’d have left all the bowls just as they were on the table,” Lisa said.

“I’ve always wondered how they managed that one bowl was too hot to eat and the next one was too cold,” her mother said.

“What I don’t understand is why did they go out for a walk when their breakfast was just ready?” Lisa said.

But when she found herself walking through the door into the bears’ kitchen, she did understand. There were the bowls of porridge on the table, one huge, one middle-sized, one tiny. The huge one was steaming hot; no one could possibly have eaten it. Obviously the Father Bear had said, “I can’t eat this, it’s far too hot to touch. Let’s go for a stroll in the forest, and I’ll have it when we get back.”

The oatmealy smell coming from the huge bowl reminded Lisa that she didn’t much care for porridge. She looked around for something else to eat.

Near the fireplace was a large wooden cupboard. It was too high up for Lisa to reach without standing on something. She looked at the huge big chair at the head of the table and pushed it with her foot. It shifted an inch or two, but it was far too heavy for her to drag right across to the cupboard. She tried the middling-sized chair. She could just move it, but it was still uncomfortably heavy. She turned to the smallest chair and managed to get it right up to the cupboard. Then she climbed up and, standing on the seat of the chair, she opened the cupboard door.

On the shelves inside were many things just like those Lisa's mother had in her kitchen cupboard: flour, sugar, salt, tea. Oats, of course. And jars and jars of honey and tins and tins of syrup. There was a tin labelled

BISCUITS. Lisa looked inside it hopefully, but it was empty. There was a round cake tin in the top far corner which Lisa could nearly, but not quite, reach. She stood on tiptoe and leaned forward so that her fingers just touched the bottom of the tin, and as she did so, the little chair tipped under her feet and Lisa fell off it on to the floor.

As she sat there, rubbing her shoulder, which was bruised, she saw with dismay that the back of the little chair had come away from the seat and that one of its legs had broken right off. What was equally bad was that Lisa had fallen across the table. The smallest bowl of porridge was lying in pieces on the floor and there was a distressing mess of porridge on the table, rapidly dripping down to join another mess on the floor.

"I'd better get out quick!" Lisa thought, and she ran to the door.

But when she looked round it, she saw, not far away, three figures coming towards the cottage from the wood.

There was a great huge figure, a middling-sized figure, and a small little tiny figure skipping around. The three bears were coming back for their breakfast.

There was nowhere in the kitchen for Lisa to hide in or behind. The only place she could escape to was up the stairs; so that was where Lisa went. Just in time. She could hear the squeals of the small little tiny bear as he came jumping along the path leading up to the front door.

Lisa looked desperately round the room in which she now found herself. There was a great huge bed, much too high for her to climb up to. There was a little bed, with its bedclothes still in a huddle. Quick as lightning, Lisa jumped into this little bed, and tried to make herself as flat as she could.

From downstairs she could hear the gruff voice of the huge bear.

"Someone's been in here while we were out," it said.

"Someone's moved my bowl of porridge," said a not-so-deep, furrier voice. It was true, Lisa had just touched the middling-sized bowl to make sure it was cold, as the story says.

"Someone's spilt my porridge all over the place and they've broken the bowl too," said a squeaky little voice. That, of course, was the little tiny bear.

"Someone's moved my chair from the head of the table," said the deep gruff voice.

"Someone's moved my chair too. I didn't leave it half across the room like that," said the furry voice, disapprovingly.

"Someone's been throwing my chair about and broken it so I can't sit in it any more," said the small squeaky voice, not sounding exactly sad about it.

"I'll mend your chair, my boy, don't worry about that," said the deep gruff voice.

"I'll make you some more porridge," said the furry voice.

"Mumma, can't I have biscuits and honey instead of porridge? Just for once?" the squeaky voice begged.

"We'd better have a look around and see who's been here," the deep gruff voice said, sounding nearer to Lisa. Could they be coming up the stairs?

"Come and eat your breakfast first. It's always the same. Just as soon as I put the food on the table, you think of something you've got to do that very minute, and then it gets cold and you complain about that," said the furry voice, scolding. Lisa heard chairs being pulled up to the table. She heard the sounds of chomping. Chump, swallow. Chump, chump, swallow. For a long time no one spoke. Lisa lay very still. Perhaps the bears would go for another walk after their meal, and then she would be able to escape.

She heard two chairs pushed back from the table. She heard a satisfied, deep belch. "Very good porridge, my dear, even if it had cooled down a trifle too much. Now let's look for whoever it was who came in here while we were out," the deep gruff voice said.

"Perhaps it was a goblin," the little squeaky voice said.

"Don't be silly, Teeny-Tiny. There's no such thing as a goblin."

"Perhaps it was a mouse."

"Oh dear! I hope not. I'm frightened of mice," the furry voice said.

"Now you're being stupid, my dear. A great, middling-sized, grown-up mother bear, frightened of mice?" the deep gruff voice said.

"They scuttle so," the furry voice said, apologetically.

"Don't tell me it was a mouse that broke Teeny-Tiny's chair."

"Teeny-Tiny, will you go upstairs for Mumma and fetch her a hankie?" the furry voice purred. Lisa heard steps coming up the stairs towards the bedroom. But Teeny-Tiny did not go to look for his mother's handkerchief. Instead he came directly over to the little bed and pulled the blankets back. He and Lisa looked at each other.

"You're not Goldilocks! Your hair is quite brown," the smallest bear said.

"How do you know about Goldilocks?" Lisa asked.

"Everyone knows about Goldilocks. Who are you?"

"I'm Lisa. I'm terribly sorry

about your porridge—"

"That's all right. I hate porridge," the smallest bear said.

"But I broke your bowl—"

"If I haven't got a bowl, Mumma can't make me eat porridge," the smallest bear said.

"And I broke your dear little chair—"

"It's too small. It's been too

small for ages. The trouble is that Mumma wants to keep me a baby, so everything I have has to be teeny-tiny. It's terrible."

From down below the furry voice floated up the stairs. "Hurry up, Teeny-Tiny. I want my handkerchief, I need to blow my nose."

"Coming at once, Mumma Bear!" the smallest bear called back. To Lisa he said, "You'd better get out before they start coming upstairs to look for you. You can get out of the window and climb down the tree outside. I've often done it while they're asleep. I'll make sure they aren't looking."

Lisa clambered out on to the

window-sill. As the littlest bear had said there was a convenient, ancient mulberry tree, asking to be climbed down, just below her. "Thank you," she said to the smallest bear.

"Any time. Come back and wreck my horrible little bed," he said. But as she ran away through the wood, Lisa thought she probably wouldn't ever go back. Here she was, running away, after escaping by the bedroom window, just as Goldilocks had. She hadn't been any cleverer, in spite of knowing the story beforehand. "Perhaps it's especially difficult with bears," Lisa thought.

The Giant Who Threw Tantrums

David Harrison

At the foot of Thistle Mountain lay a village.

In the village lived a little boy who liked to go walking. One Saturday afternoon he was walking in the woods when he was startled by a terrible noise.

He scrambled behind a bush.

Before long a huge giant came

stamping down the path.

He looked upset.

"Tanglebangled ringlepox!" the giant bellowed. He banged his head against a tree until the leaves shook off like snowflakes.

"Franglewhangled whippersnack!" the giant roared. Yanking up the tree, he whirled it around his head and knocked down twenty-seven other trees.

Muttering to himself, he stalked up the path towards the top of Thistle Mountain.

The little boy hurried home.

"I just saw a giant throwing a tantrum!" he told everyone in the village.

They only smiled.

"There's no such thing as a giant," the mayor assured him.

"He knocked down twenty-seven trees," said the little boy.

"Must have been a tornado," the weatherman said with a nod. "Happens around here all the time."

The next Saturday afternoon the little boy again went walking. Before long he heard a horrible noise. Quick as lightning, he slipped behind a tree.

Soon the same giant came storming down the path. He still looked upset.

"Pollywogging frizzelsnatch!" he

yelled. Throwing himself down, he pounded the ground with both fists.

Boulders bounced like hailstones.

Scowling, the giant puckered his lips into an "O".

He drew in his breath sharply. It sounded like somebody slurping soup. "Pooh!" he cried. Grabbing

his left foot with both hands, the giant hopped on his right foot up the path towards the top of Thistle Mountain. The little boy hurried home.

"That giant's at it again," he told everyone. "He threw such a tantrum that the ground trembled!"

"Must have been an earthquake," the police chief said. "Happens around here sometimes."

The next Saturday afternoon the little boy again went walking. Before long he heard a frightening noise.

He dropped down behind a rock.

Soon the giant came fuming

down the path. When he reached the little boy's rock, he puckered his lips into an "O". He drew in his breath sharply with a loud, rushing-wind sound. "Phooey!" he cried. "I *never* get it right!"

The giant held his breath until his face turned blue and his eyes rolled up. "Fozzlehumper backawacket!" he panted. Then he lumbered up the path towards the top of Thistle Mountain.

The little boy followed him. Up and up and up he climbed to the very top of Thistle Mountain.

There he discovered a huge cave. A surprising sound was coming from it. The giant was crying!

"All I want is to whistle," he sighed through his tears. "But every time I try, it comes out wrong!"

The little boy had just learned to whistle. He knew how hard it could be. He stepped into the cave.

The giant looked surprised. "How did *you* get here?"

"I know what you're doing wrong," the little boy said.

When the giant heard that, he leaned down and put his hands on his knees.

"Tell me at once!" he begged.

"You have to stop throwing tantrums," the little boy told him.

"I promise!" said the giant, who

didn't want anyone to think he had poor manners.

"Pucker your lips—" the little boy said.

"I always do!" the giant assured him.

"Then blow," the little boy added.

"Blow?"

"Blow."

The giant looked as if he didn't believe it. He puckered his lips into an "O". He blew. Out came a long, low whistle. It sounded like a railway engine. The giant smiled.

He shouted, "I whistled! Did you hear that? I whistled!"

Taking the little boy's hand, he danced in a circle.

"You're a good friend," the giant said.

"Thank you," said the little boy. "Perhaps some time we can whistle together. But just now I have to go. It's my suppertime."

The giant stood before his cave and waved goodbye.

The little boy seldom saw the giant after that. But the giant kept his promise about not throwing tantrums.

"We never have earthquakes," the mayor liked to say.

"Haven't had a tornado in ages," the weatherman would add.

Now and then they heard a long, low whistle somewhere in the distance.

"Must be a train," the police chief would say.

But the little boy knew his friend the giant was walking up the path towards the top of Thistle Mountain – whistling.

Tim's Tooth

Heather Eyles

Tim had a wobbly tooth. It had been wobbling for weeks. Every day when he felt it with his tongue it wobbled a little bit more, until it seemed as if it was only hanging on by the merest thread.

Tim was impatient to lose his tooth, but he didn't dare pull it out himself. He had never lost a tooth before.

Tim knew he would get some

money for his tooth.

"How much?" he asked his mum.

"Oh, I don't know," she would say, "I expect that depends on how rich the tooth fairy is feeling. How about fifty pence?"

Tim thought that was quite a good deal, and he would push the tooth even harder with his tongue (it was a bottom one, at the very front) but it still didn't fall out.

"Pull it!" said his sister Sally. "Just get a hold of it and yank! I'll do it for you if you like!"

"Get off!" said Tim, "It's my tooth and I'm waiting for it to fall out by itself."

"Baby!" said his sister, but Tim

noticed she wasn't too keen on pulling her own loose teeth out.

One day at playtime Tim was swinging as usual on the climbing frame, which was his favourite place to be, when – BOING! – a big boy's foot swung right into him and sloshed him straight in the face. It was an accident, of course, but it made Tim cry, and when he'd stopped crying and felt his face to see if it was all right, he realised his tooth was missing.

His precious tooth! His tooth was worth fifty pence!

It was enough to make him start crying all over again, but when the playtime lady asked him what the matter was, he told her, and soon she had the whole playground crawling around on their hands and knees looking for Tim's tooth. His best friend Harry discovered it, under one of the benches at the side of the playground. It had flown out of his mouth and rolled all that way!

It was so tiny, just a little white pearl with a rough bit and a speck of blood at one end, not like a tooth at all. But Tim had it back and that was the important thing.

He felt the place where it had been very gingerly. It felt all soft and squidgy and tasted a little of blood. Tim didn't like that much, but he was so proud of his tooth it didn't matter and he knew there'd be a new tooth growing there soon.

The playtime lady, who was called Mrs Gibbons, found him a little piece of tissue paper to wrap his tooth up in.

"Now keep it safe," she said, "or

the tooth fairy won't leave you any money!"

"I'm going to get fifty pence!" said Tim proudly.

"Well I never!" said Mrs Gibbons, "that's just what my children get. But for their very first tooth they always get a pound."

"Do they?" wondered Tim. "A whole pound?"

"Only for the first one," said Mrs Gibbons, "fifty pence after that."

Tim thought about that all the way through his lessons. In fact, I don't think he did any lessons at all that day, he was thinking so much about the money he was going to get for his tooth. Every so often he would put his hand in his pocket and feel the little wad of tissue paper, just to make sure it was still there. Once or twice he unwrapped it in the classroom and laid the tooth on his table to admire it, but as it was so small it was so easy to lose and once it rolled right off the table and he thought he'd lost it again, until he found it under his teacher's chair. After that he didn't take it out of its packet again.

He didn't even show it to Aunty Barbara when she came to pick him up after school, for fear he would lose it again. He was saving it up to show his mum. And his dad of course, and his horrible sister. He'd tell her he'd pulled it out himself, not that someone had kicked it out for him!

When his mum came to pick him up from Aunty Barbara's he was so excited he could hardly speak.

"Mum, Mum, look!" he said, and he took it very carefully out of his pocket and slowly unravelled the tissue paper for her to see.

"Oh!" she said, "how wonderful, Tim! I was wondering when that was going to come out. That's worth fifty pence tonight."

Tim looked at his mum very hard. "Mrs Gibbons says that the

tooth fairy gives her children one pound for their very first tooth. A whole pound!"

Tim's mum frowned. "A pound? That sounds a lot."

"Only for the first one. After that they get fifty pence."

"We'll see," she said. "Let's hope the tooth fairy's feeling rich tonight."

You can imagine what Sally said when she heard Tim was hoping for a whole pound for his tooth.

"That's not fair! I only got fifty pence for my teeth! He can't have a pound!"

"Oh, for goodness sake, you two," said Mum, who was extremely busy making sandwiches for a meeting they were having in their living room that night. "It's really not important!"

"It is!" cried Sally. "It's not fair and that's important!"

"Oh Sally, I'll give you fifty pence if that makes you happier. All this fuss about a poor little tooth. You'll drive me mad, you children!"

Tim could see that his mum was very busy buttering and slicing, so he decided to put himself to bed. He cleaned his remaining teeth, taking care to avoid the hole where his old tooth had been, and he got into his pyjamas. People were already knocking at the door for the meeting, so his mum and dad hardly noticed him go up. Right at the very top of the stairs, outside his bedroom, Tim unwrapped the little packet of tissue paper for the very last time. There it was, the precious tooth. He bent his head for a closer look, he breathed on it.

All of a sudden the tooth rolled right off the tissue paper, right off his hand and began to roll down the stairs. Tim couldn't move. He saw the tooth come to rest right by a small hole in the floorboards where a mouse used to live until a man from the council came and got rid of it. Tim padded down the stairs after his tooth. He put out his fingers very carefully like a pair of tweezers to pick it up. Then, "What are you doing?"

Tim jumped. It was Sally. Tim looked round at her crossly. When he looked back the tooth had gone.

He had accidentally knocked it down the hole in the floorboards!

"It's only an old mousehole," said Sally. "What are you staring at it for?"

"Nothing!" said Tim. He wasn't going to tell her he'd lost his tooth.

Nor could he tell his mum and dad. The door to the living room was firmly shut and they'd be deep in their meeting by now. Maybe it didn't matter. Maybe the tooth fairy would come anyway, tooth or no tooth. Tim certainly hoped so. But he wasn't going to tell Sally, oh no!

In the morning the first thing

Tim did was feel under his pillow. He expected to feel something hard and round and shiny. There was nothing. He lifted the pillow. Still nothing. The tooth fairy hadn't been. Disappointed, he tiptoed into his parents' room.

"Ummmmm," said his mum, half asleep. "What is it?"

"Mum," said Tim, climbing in under the duvet, "the tooth fairy didn't come."

"What?" said his mum, suddenly waking up and sitting up very quickly. "Oh dear! Oh dear, Tim. I am sorry. She must have forgotten. I know, perhaps she'll come tonight instead."

"She won't," Tim said sadly. "You see, I lost the tooth."

"You lost it?"

"I dropped it down a hole in the floorboards. I can't reach it to get it back."

"I see," said his mum, settling back on to the pillows, "well that explains why she didn't come. You have to have a tooth to show her. As proof."

"Does that mean I shan't get my money?"

"Well," said his mum, "I suppose I could give you the money instead, as I know you really did lose the tooth."

Tim thought about it.

"It's not the same," he said. "It's not the same at all. I want the tooth fairy to give it to me."

"I'll think about what to do," said his mum.

Tim didn't have a very good day at school that day. Everybody kept asking him if he'd got money for his tooth, and he got fed up with explaining about the hole in the floorboards. Mrs Gibbons was the worst.

"After all that trouble we went to," she said, "and we spent ages looking for it. If I was your mummy, I'd write the tooth fairy a note."

"What kind of note?" asked Tim.

"Well, I'd write a note to the fairy, saying that Tim had lost a tooth and it was down a hole in the floorboards. Then you'd get your money after all."

"Right!" said Tim.

He couldn't wait to tell his mum his idea. After tea he fetched a pen and some paper and put it in front of her.

"Write a letter," he said. "To the tooth fairy. Mrs Gibbons says it's just as good."

"Does she?" said Mum. "Mrs Gibbons seems to be full of bright ideas."

"I don't think he should have any money at all," said Sally, "it's his fault if he lost it. And he's only to get fifty pence!"

"Now, let me see . . ." said his mum. And this is what she wrote.

DEAR TOOTH FAIRY,

THIS IS TO CERTIFY THAT TIM REALLY DID LOSE A TOOTH AND THAT IT ROLLED DOWN A HOLE IN THE FLOORBOARDS AND CAN'T BE RETRIEVED. IF YOU WANT TO VERIFY THIS, THE HOLE IS AT THE BOTTOM OF THE STAIRS, ON THE RIGHT HAND SIDE.

SIGNED

Mum

"Is that OK?"

"Great!" said Tim.

That night he went to bed with his note tucked under his pillow. His mum and dad didn't have a meeting that night, so they were able to read him a bedtime story and give him a kiss and things were all round much nicer. Even Sally was in a good mood as Dad had given her an extra fifty pence pocket money.

Tim couldn't wait till morning.

He woke at daybreak, and remembering straight away he slipped his hand under his pillow. Nothing on that side.

He tried the other side. Nothing

there either.

His heart sinking he lifted up the whole pillow.

Right in the middle, underneath, was a bright, shiny, new pound coin, winking at him in the sunlight.

And beside it, guess what, there was his small, white, pearly tooth.

Sam Pig Seeks His Fortune

Alison Uttley

One day Sam Pig started out to seek his fortune, and this was the reason. He came down as usual for breakfast, with never a thought except that he was hungry and there was a larder full of food. It was a sunny morning and he decided he would bask in the garden, and enjoy himself, and do nothing at all.

"Go and fill the kettle at the spring," said Ann, when he entered the room. He picked up the copper kettle and carried it down the lane to the spring of water which gushed out of the earth. Then he staggered slowly back, spilling all the way.

"That's my day's work done," he said to himself as he lifted it to the fire.

"Go and chop some sticks, Sam," said Bill, when he was comfortably settled at the table. He picked up the axe from the corner and went to the woodstack. Then he chipped and he chopped till he had a fine pile of kindling. He filled the wood-box and brought it back to the house.

"That's two days' work done," said he to himself as he put some of the wood under the kettle. He returned to his seat but Ann called him again.

"Blow up the fire, Sam," she ordered. He reached down the blow-bellows and he puffed and he huffed and he blew out his own fat cheeks as well as the bellows. Then the fire crackled and a spurt of flame roared out and the kettle began to sing.

"That's three days' work done," said Sam to himself and he listened to the kettle's song, and tried to find out what it said.

"Go and fetch the eggs, Sam," said Tom, and away he went once more. He chased the hens out of the garden and hunted under the hedgeside for the eggs. He put them in a rhubarb-leaf basket and walked slowly back to the house. His legs were tired already, and he looked very cross.

"That's four days' work done," said he to himself, and he put the basket on the table. Then he sat down and waited for breakfast, but Ann called him once more.

"Sam. Wash your face and brush your hair," she said. "How can you sit down like a piggy-pig?"

That settled it! To be called a piggy-pig was the last straw! All Sam's plans suddenly changed. His life was going to be different. He had had enough of family rule.

"I'm going to seek my fortune," he announced loudly, when he had scrubbed his face and hands and brushed his bristly hair. "I'm going off right away after breakfast to seek my fortune."

He put a handful of sugar in his cup and blew on his tea and supped his porridge noisily, in defiant mood.

"And what may that be?" asked Bill sarcastically. "What is your fortune, Sam?"

"His face is his fortune," said Tom, rudely.

"You foolish young pig," cried Ann. "What would Badger say? You must stay at home and help us. We can't do without you."

"I know you can't." Sam tossed his head. "That's why I'm going." And he ate his breakfast greedily, for he didn't know when he would have another as good.

He took his knapsack from the wall and put in it a loaf of bread and a round cheese. He brushed his small hooves and stuck a feather in his hat. Then he cut a stick from the hazel tree and away he went.

"Goodbye," he called, waving his hat to his astonished sister and brothers. "Goodbye, I shall return rich and great some day."

"Goodbye. You'll soon come running back, Brother Sam," they laughed.

Now he hadn't gone far when he heard a mooing in some bushes.

"Moo! Moo! Moo!"

He turned aside and there was a poor lone cow caught by her horns, struggling to free herself. He unfastened the boughs and pulled the branches apart so that the cow could get away.

"Thank you. Thank you," said the cow. "Where are you going

so early, Sam Pig?"

"To seek my fortune," said Sam.

"Then let me go with you," said the cow. "We shall be company." So the cow and Sam went along together, the cow ambling slowly, eating as she walked, Sam Pig trying to hurry her.

"Take a lift on my back," said the cow kindly, and Sam leaped up to her warm comfortable back. There he perched himself with his little legs astride and his tail curled up.

They went through woods and along lanes. Sam stared about from the cow's back, seeking his fortune everywhere.

"Miaow! Miaow!" The cry came

from a tree, and Sam looked up in surprise. On a high bough sat a white cat, wailing in misery.

"What is the matter?" asked Sam.

"I've got up here," sobbed the white cat, "and I can't get down. I've been here for two nights and a day, and nobody has helped me. There are boogles and witches about in the night, and I'm scared out of my seven wits."

"I'll get you down," said Sam Pig proudly, and he stood on the cow's head and reached up with his hazel switch. The white cat slithered along it and slipped safely to the ground.

"Oh, thank you! Thank you, kind

sir," said the cat. "I'll go with you, wherever you go," said she.

"I'm going to seek my fortune," said Sam.

"Then I'll go too," said the white cat, and she walked behind the cow with her tail upright like a flag and her feet stepping delicately and finely.

Away they went to seek Sam's fortune, and they hadn't gone far when they heard a dog barking.

"Bow wow. Bow wow," it said.

The cow turned aside and the cat followed, after a natural hesitation.

In a field they saw a poor thin dog with its foot caught in a trap. The cow forced the trap open and released the creature. Away it limped, holding up its paw, but Sam put a dock-leaf bandage upon it, and bound it with ribbons of grasses.

"I'll come with you," said the dog gratefully. "I'll follow you, kind sir."

"I'm going to seek my fortune," said Sam.

"Then I'll go too," barked the dog, and it followed after. But the white cat changed her place and sprang between the cow's horns; and that's the way they went, the cow with Sam on her back and the cat between her horns and the lame dog trotting behind.

Now after a time they heard a squeaking and a squawking from the hedgeside. There was a little Jenny Wren, struggling for its life in a bird-net.

"What's the matter?" asked Sam.

"I'm caught in this net and if nobody rescues me, I shall die," cried the trembling wren.

"I'll save you," said Sam, and he tore open the meshes of the net and freed the little bird.

"Oh, thank you. Thank you," said the wren. "I'll go with you wherever you go."

Then it saw the green eyes of the cat watching it from the cow's horns, so it flew to the other end of the cow and perched on its tail. Away they all went, the cow with the pig on her back and the cat on her horns and the bird on her tail, and behind walked the dog.

They went along the woods and meadows, always seeking Sam's fortune. After a time it began to rain and they got bedraggled and wet. Then out came the sun and they saw a great rainbow stretching across the sky and dipping down to the field where they walked. The beautiful arch touched the earth at an old twisty hawthorn tree.

"That's where my fortune is hidden," cried Sam, pointing to

the thorn bush. "At the foot of the rainbow, Badger told me once to look there. 'Seek at the foot of a rainbow and you'll find a fortune,' he said to me, and there's the rainbow pointing to the ground!"

So down they scrambled: the white cat leaped from the cow's horns, Sam sidled from the cow's back and the bird flew down from the cow's tail. They all began to dig and to rootle with horns and feet and bill and claws and snout. They tossed away the black earth and dug into the crumpled roots of the tree. There lay a crock filled with pieces of gold.

"Here's my fortune," cried Sam Pig, lifting it out.

"We can't eat it," said the cow, snuffling at it with her wet nose. "It's hard as stone."

"We can't eat it," said the white cat, putting out a delicate pink tongue. "It's tough as wood."

"We can't eat it," barked the dog, biting with sharp teeth at the gold. "It's harsh as rocks."

"We can't eat it," sang the bird, pecking at the pieces. "It's cruel as a snare."

"What use is your fortune?" they all asked Sam.

"I don't know." Sam shook his head and scratched himself behind the ear. "I've found it, and that is what I set out to do."

"I'm weary," said the cow. "Let us stay here all night."

The cow began to crop the grass, and the cat supped the bowl of milk which the cow gave to it. The bird found a few fat worms where the earth had been disturbed. As for Sam, he shared his bread and cheese with the dog, and all were satisfied and at peace with one another. The cow tucked her legs under her big body and bowed her head in sleep. The cat curled up in a white ball. The wren put its head under its wing. The dog rested with its chin on its paws.

Then Sam cut a stick from the hawthorn tree. It was a knobby thorn full of magic, for it had guarded the gold for a thousand years, ever since the fairies had hidden it. Of course Sam didn't know that, but Badger would have warned him if he had been there.

"Never cut a bough from a twisty ancient thorn," he would have said. "There's a power of magic hidden in it."

Sam cut the thorn and trimmed it with his clasp knife, and leaned it up against the tree over the crock of gold, all ready to catch a robber if one should come in the night. Then he lay down next to the dog.

The moon came up in the sky and looked at the strange assembly under the old hawthorn tree. She blinked through the branches of the old thorn and shot her moonbeams at the cudgel, shaking it into life. Slowly it rose and staggered across the grass. Then it began to belabour every creature there except the little wren which was asleep in the tree.

When the cow felt the sharp blows across her ribs, she turned on the dog and tossed it with her sharp horns. The dog rushed at the cat and tried to worry it. The cat scrambled up the tree and tried to catch the bird. The little Jenny Wren awoke with a cry and flew away.

Sam took to his heels and ran as fast as he could along the lanes and through the woods and across the meadows till he reached home. He banged at the door and woke them all up.

"Where's the fortune, Sam?" asked Bill and Tom and little Ann Pig. "Did you find a crock of gold?"

"Yes. A crock of gold," cried Sam, out of breath with running so fast. "A crock of gold under the rainbow end."

"Where is it?" they asked. "Gold is useful sometimes and it would do fine to mend the hole in our roof. Where is it, Sam?"

Then Sam told how he had found the gold under the hawthorn tree, but the tree had belaboured them soundly in the night and he had run home.

"That gold is bewitched," said Ann. "Best leave it where you found it."

"I would like to see the crock of gold, and touch it, and smell it," interrupted Bill.

"So would I," added Tom. "I've never seen any gold."

"Then I will take you there tomorrow after I've had a good sleep," yawned Sam. "That is if you don't make me work before breakfast."

The next morning they all went across the wood and over the meadows to the old hawthorn tree where Sam had found the crock of gold.

A cow was feeding in the thick grass of the field, and a white cat was leaning with her paw outstretched over the stream fishing for minnows. A dog chased a rabbit through the hedge and a little Jenny Wren piped and sang.

There was no crock of gold anywhere to be seen, but underneath the old bent tree grew a host of king-cups, glittering like gold pence in the sunlight, fluttering their yellow petals in their dark green leaves.

"You imagined the gold," said Bill indignantly. "You've led us here on a wild goose chase," and he cuffed poor Sam Pig over the head.

"I didn't!" protested Sam. "There's the cudgel I cut from the tree."

On the ground lay a thick stick, knotted and thorny and dark. The pigs leaned over it without touching it; then they began to gather the flowers.

"Quite true," they nodded. "Quite true, Sam Pig. You did find a fortune after all. There it lies, all turned into yellow flowers, much more use than metal to a family of pigs. Let the human kind take the hard metal, and we'll take the posies. King-cups are good for pains and aches; their seeds make pills and their leaves are cool poultices and their flowers are a delight to our sharp noses."

They gathered a bunch and walked slowly home through the fresh fields wet with dew. All the way they talked to Sam kindly and treated him as if he had indeed brought a fortune to them.

"Badger will be pleased with you, little Pig-wiggin," said they and this was high praise for little Sam Pig.

The Boy With Two Shadows

Margaret Mahy

There was a little boy who took great care of his shadow. He was quite a careful little boy with his buttons and shoes and all the odd pieces. But most especially he was careful with his shadow because he knew he had only one, and it had to last him his life. He always tried to manage things so that his shadow didn't trail in the dust, and if he just couldn't keep it out of the dust he hurried to get to a clean place for it.

This boy took such care of his shadow that a witch noticed it. She stopped the boy on his way home from school.

"I've been watching you," she said. "I like the way you look after your shadow."

"Well," said the boy, trying to sound grown-up, "the way I see it is this – it's the only one I've got. And it's going to have to last me a long time."

"True! True!" said the witch, looking at him with great

approval. "You're the lad for me. The thing is, I want someone to look after *my* shadow while I am away on holiday. I don't want to drag that skinny old thing around with me. You know what a nuisance a shadow can be."

"Mine isn't any trouble," said the boy doubtfully.

"That's as may be," the witch declared. "The thing is, I want to be rid of mine for two weeks but I'm not going to leave it with just anybody – it's going to be left with *you*."

The boy didn't like to argue with a witch.

"All right," he said, "but hurry

back, won't you?"

The witch bared her teeth in a witch smile, which was quite wicked-looking, though she was trying to be pleasant.

"If you return my shadow in good condition," she promised, "you shall have a magic spell all of your own. I'll choose just the right one for you." Then she fastened her shadow onto the boy's shadow, got on her broom, and made off, light and free as thistledown, with sunlight all around her and no bobbling black patch chasing at her heels.

The boy now had two shadows. One was his own. The other was

the fierce, crooked, thorny shadow of the witch.

The boy had nothing but trouble with that witch's shadow. It was the worst behaved shadow in the world! Usually, it is a rule that shadows behave much as their people do – but the witch's wouldn't do that. When the little boy went to buy apples the witch's shadow rummaged among the shadows of the fruit. It put the shadows of all the oranges over beside the bananas, and mixed up the shadows of the peaches. Everything was all higgledy-piggledy.

The man in the fruit shop said, "Throw that shadow out! How on earth am I going to sell oranges when they've got no shadows? And who's going to buy bananas with the shadows of oranges?"

The little boy didn't like to turn the witch's shadow loose on its own. He rushed out of the shop without his apples.

At home, all through tea, the witch's shadow stretched itself long and leaped all over the wall. It took the shadow from the clock, and the clock stopped. Then it terrified the parrot into fits, and pulled the shadow-tail of the dog's shadow.

"Really!" said the little boy's mother. "I can't enjoy my tea with that ugly thing waltzing around the walls! You'll have to keep it outside."

But the boy was determined to look after the witch's shadow. From then on, he had his tea in the kitchen on his own. He got so clever at keeping the witch's shadow from getting into mischief and wickedness that at last it couldn't find anything wicked to do. Naturally this made it very cross.

Then suddenly, in spite of the little boy's care, the shadow thought of something new and mean – so mean that you would think even a witch's shadow would be ashamed. It started to pinch and tease and bite and haunt the little boy's *own* shadow. It was terrible to see. The boy's shadow had always been treated kindly. His own shadow did not know what to do now about this new, fierce thing that tormented it, pushed it onto dusty places and trod on its heels as they hurried down the road.

One day the boy's shadow could bear this no longer. In broad daylight the boy, going home to lunch, saw his two shadows – short and squat – running beside

him. He saw the witch's shadow nip his own smaller shadow with her long witch fingernails. His own shadow gave a great bound and broke away from his feet. Down the road it flew, like a great black beetle or a bit of waste paper flapping in the wind, then it was gone. The little boy ran after it, but it was nowhere to be seen. He stood still and listened to the warm summer afternoon. It was so quiet he could hear the witch shadow laughing – or rather, he heard the echo of laughing. (Because, as you know, an echo is the shadow of a sound, and sometimes the sound of a shadow.)

Well, you can just imagine. There was the little boy with only one shadow again – but it was the *wrong* shadow. His real shadow was quite gone, and now he had only the witch's left.

It was more like having a thorn bush at his heels than a proper shadow. There was nothing comfortable about this, and people stared and nudged one another.

As for the boy, he felt sad and lonely without his own shadow. He tried to like the witch's shadow, and he tried hard to take good care of it – but it was a thankless task. You might just as well try to pet a wild she-wolf or a thistle!

At last the witch came back. She wrote the boy a letter in grey ink on black paper, telling him to meet her that night at midnight and to be sure to bring her shadow with him. (Thank goodness it was a bright moonlit night or it might have been extremely difficult to find that wretched shadow, which hid away from him sometimes.) As it was, the witch whisked it back in half a minute less than no time. (In fact, it didn't even take her as long as that.)

"Now," the witch said very craftily, "here's your spell." She handed the boy a small striped pill, wrapped in a bat's wing.

"It's one I don't use much myself," she said. "But the boy who swallows that pill can turn himself into a camel. *Any* sort of camel, even a white racing camel – or a Bactrian or any sort of camel you like."

The little boy couldn't help feeling it was a bit useless, in a way, to be able to turn himself into a camel. What he really wanted was just his own shadow back. He pointed out to the witch that her fierce shadow had driven his own gentle one away. The witch sniggered a bit in a witch-like, but very irritating, fashion.

"Well, my dear," she said, "you

can't expect everything to be easy, you know. Anyhow, I feel I've paid you handsomely for your trouble. Run off home now."

The boy *had* to do what he was told. He scuttled off sadly down the street to his home, carefully holding down the pocket where he had put the striped pill. It was bright moonlight and everything had its shadow – the trees trailed theirs out over the road, the fence posts pointed theirs across the paddocks. The sleeping cows had sleeping shadows tucked in beside them. Only the little boy had no shadow. He felt very lonely.

At the gate to his house he

thought at first that his mother was waiting for him. A dim figure seemed to be watching out, peering up the road. But it wasn't tall enough to be his mother, and besides, when he looked again it wasn't there. Then something moved without any sound. He looked again. Softly and shyly as if it was ashamed of itself, his own shadow slid out from among the other shadows, and sidled toward him. It slipped along, toe-to-toe with him, just as it had always done.

The little boy thought for a moment: He was free of the witch's shadow.

He had a magic trick that would turn him into any sort of camel he liked – if he ever wanted to.

And now he had his own shadow back again!

Everything had turned out for the best. He was so pleased he did a strange little dance in the moonlight, while, toe-to-toe, his shadow danced beside him.

The Magic Broom

Anonymous

Phillipippa was the kitchen-maid in King Carraway's palace. She washed the royal dishes, peeled the royal potatoes, and swept the red-tiled floor of the royal kitchen.

She did many other things besides these, but it would take far too long to write them all down here.

One morning the cook sent her

to market to buy a new broom.

"That old one is a perfect disgrace to the royal household; you must have a new one at once," said she crossly.

"Yes, Ma'am," replied Phillipippa, "I'll go at once."

She always said Ma'am when speaking to the cook, as it helped to keep her in a good temper. Phillipippa was very tactful.

The cook was fat. Her cotton print dresses were so tight that they looked as if the buttons might burst at any moment. Phillipippa felt quite nervous about it sometimes.

It didn't take her very long to get

to the market-place. She tried several stalls, but couldn't buy a broom anywhere. They had all sold out. Phillipippa stood in the middle of the market square and debated what to do. She dare not go back to the royal palace without a broom. It was very awkward indeed.

Just at that moment along came a pedlar, and under his arm was the most beautiful broom Phillipippa had ever set eyes upon!

"Oh! what a love!" she exclaimed. "Please, is it for sale?"

"Yes," said the pedlar. He didn't tell her that he had picked it up in the road that very morning!

Phillipippa bought the broom and hurried back to the royal palace as fast as she could go.

"My word! What a time you've been!" said the cook.

"Indeed, Ma'am, I—"

"That is quite enough from you, Miss, thank you. And don't stand there staring either; anybody would think we had nothing to do. Come and sweep up the kitchen at once! I've been making the stuffing for the royal goose, and the crumbs have gone all over the floor." The cook snatched up an oven-cloth and banged a saucepan down on the fire with a bump, so that the coals scattered in all directions!

"My! *What* a temper she's got!" thought Phillipippa.

She picked up her new broom and began sweeping the floor. Over the red tiles flew the broom, swish, swish! She had no sooner began than she had finished! Phillipippa stared in amazement. What a wonderful broom it was! So light! She had never swept the kichen floor as quickly as *that* before! It must be enchanted!

"Well, if that isn't luck!" thought Phillipippa. "We're going to be great friends, I can see," she said, patting the broom handle affectionately.

Next day, quite early, a little old

woman came knocking at the kitchen door.

Phillipippa was sweeping round the royal larder. She unfastened the door.

"Good morning to you, Miss," said the little old woman. "May I ask what you are doing with my broom?"

"*Your* broom?" cried the astonished Phillipippa. "Why, I bought it myself in the market yesterday."

"So you may have," replied the old woman angrily, "but I tell you it's *my* broom, just the same."

"Well, and what about me?" the broom asked suddenly in a little, high, squeaky voice.

Phillipippa was so surprised that she let go the broom handle with a jerk. It didn't fall over, but stood up all by itself in the middle of the floor!

"Come home *at once*," cackled the witch. "How *dare* you run away like that!"

"You run away yourself," piped the broom, "you horrid old woman! I'm quite happy where I am, thank you."

"Oh, are you?" cried the witch. "We'll soon see who is the master here!"

"Oh, shall we?" retorted the broom, and it shook all over with rage. "Go away at once," it squeaked, "or I'll sweep you out!"

"I don't think I should do that," said Phillipippa, beginning to feel quite alarmed.

But she had no sooner spoken, than the broom began sweeping as hard as it could go. Out of the royal kitchen it swept the old woman, and across the courtyard, so that she had to pick up her petticoats and run. Swish, swish, swish!

Over the drawbridge ran the witch, with the broom close at her heels.

And then, all of a sudden, the broom was back again in

Phillipippa's hand, just as if nothing at all had happened! And as for the little old woman, she was nowhere to be seen!

"Well, if that isn't strange!" thought Phillipippa. But she never said one word about it to anybody.

The Gigantic Badness

Janet McNeill

Nobody blamed the Giant for his bigness – a giant can't help being big – but the badness of the Giant was certainly his fault, everyone in the town and countryside was sure about that.

"He's bad, that Giant is," they grumbled, shaking their heads when they found huge footprints sunk deep on newly sown fields of corn, or hedges squashed flat.

"Never a thought for anyone but himself," they growled if the Giant sang songs late into the night when everyone else wanted to get to sleep, or when he burnt his toast and the smell hung about the air for a couple of days. "He's a rogue for sure," they complained, "if it isn't one thing it's another."

And sometimes they forgot to scold their children for talking with their mouths full, or coming into the house without wiping their feet, or sitting down at the table before their hands were washed, because these were such small badnesses, compared with the enormous outsize badness of the Giant.

Tom was one of the smallest boys in the town and he certainly wasn't the best behaved. He envied the giant, both for his size and his badness. When you are as large as a giant there are a great many extra ways of being bad and the Giant tried most of them. He lived over the hill behind the town, but sometimes he crossed the field where the saw-mill was and if the smoke was coming out of the tall chimney he leaned over and blew down it so that the men who were working in the mill coughed and spluttered.

Sometimes in the early morning

he reached a finger to the school house bell hanging high against the roof, and all the children, halfway through their breakfasts, gulped and gobbled and raced into school half an hour early.

Once when Tom was sailing his boats in the river the Giant decided it was a good day to take a swim farther upstream, and he enjoyed it so much that he lay on his back, kicking and splashing. Water rose up around him in fountains and then poured downstream in great waves, so that Tom's boats were swamped, and those that didn't sink were tossed against the bank with their rigging tangled and the thin stick masts smashed into pieces.

That was bad enough, but a week later while Tom was out on the hill flying his new kite the Giant walked by, tangling the string of the kite in his bootlaces so that it came down in the middle of a gorse bush, all torn and broken.

Tom picked up the bits and carried them home. "I'll get even with that Giant, see if I don't," he growled all the way down the hill, and the wind heard him and laughed, "Get even with the Giant! I'd like to see you manage it! What would you do, a boy your size, a button of a boy, a pinhole person, what could you do to beat a Giant as big and as bad as that Giant is?"

"You wait and see," Tom promised, "just wait! I may not be big but I know how to be bad!"

But what could he do? Perhaps the wind had been right. Tom thought about it for a week. One day when school was over he went across the hill into the valley where the Giant lived. He had never been there before. It was a bare, grey, lonely place, rocks, little grass, and one tall leafless tree at the dark entrance where the Giant made his home.

Tom decided to hide behind a

rock and wait for the Giant. The sun had gone down, the shadows were long and blue and there was a cool moon in the sky when the Giant came home. He tramped up the valley whistling a tune to himself, and the noise he made was as loud as the town's flute band when they were out on parade. When he reached the mouth of the cave the Giant kicked off his boots, one first and then the other, hung his shabby hat on the top of the tree and went into the cave for supper and his bed.

Tom tiptoed out from behind the rock. He stared up at the Giant's hat. It was the size of a bath. Even if he did get up to the top of the tree there would be no chance of shifting it. He leaned over the edge of one of the boots. “He wouldn’t go far without these,” he decided, and he put one of the laces over his shoulder and bent his back and heaved. But it was no use, the Giant’s boot was so heavy that Tom couldn’t budge it an inch.

“No use,” teased the wind, “no use at all. What can you do, a feather-boned boy the size of you?”

But Tom had an idea. Glue was what he needed and his father was a carpenter so he knew where glue could be found. The following evening after it was dark Tom carried a pot of glue into the Giant's valley. The boots were there. Tom emptied half of the pot of glue into one boot and half into the other and went off home to bed.

Next morning what a commotion from the other side of the hill, what a stamping and a thumping, what a roaring and a bellowing! It went on all day, so that no one in the town heard the church clock chiming or the school bell ringing, and not a single hen in any henhouse laid a single egg. It was late in the evening and the townspeople were almost distracted when they heard first one tremendous crash and then another, then a sigh like a steam engine blowing off steam, and after that silence. "I wonder what all that was about," they said to each other as they collected the babies and put them to bed. Tom smiled. He knew.

That night the wind whistled down his bedroom chimney, "Bully for you, Tom, bully for you, bully for yoo-oo-ou!"

"I told you, didn't I?" Tom said, and he put his head below the blankets and went to sleep.

For several weeks no one heard much of the giant. "He's lying low," they said to each other. "He's run out of ideas," Tom said to himself. Saturday was the day of the big cricket match, the boys from Tom's town were playing the boys from a town nearby. It was always a very important day, and specially important this year for Tom because he had been chosen to play in the team. He ached for the feeling of the bat in his hands. This would be a day for lifting the ball high into the sky. What a match this was going to be! The teams with their supporters trooped up to the cricket pitch.

But the Giant had got there first. There he was, stretched out at his ease from one side of the pitch to the other. That was how they found him, very peaceful and comfortable, his hands clasped behind his head, one foot across the other. His eyes were closed, he was fast asleep!

They shouted and they yelled and the Giant woke up but didn't move. They tried arguing. The Headmaster of the school appealed to the Giant's better feelings. "Better feelings? Never heard of them," the Giant said and plucked up a cricket stump to use as a toothpick. The boldest of the boys poked and prodded, but it was no use. How could anyone play cricket with a giant lying in the way? And to make it worse the Giant had fallen asleep again.

"Now what'll you do? Now what'll you-oo-oo-ou do-oo-oo?" whistled the wind in Tom's ears. And Tom knew exactly what to do. He passed the word around and in no time at all the fire brigade arrived with their hoses, and it wasn't long before a drenched and dripping Giant, a gasping, soaked, indignant Giant was on his feet and off up the hill with the water running down his neck and out of his ears.

So the match was played and Tom was the hero of the day, both for the runs he scored and for the way he had got the better of the Giant. “Beautiful,” the wind said that evening, ruffling his bedroom curtains, “beau-eau-eau-tiful!”

But the Giant caught a cold from his wetting and he wasn’t the only one to suffer from it; all the next week the town was shaken by his enormous sneezes, windows rattled, doors came unlatched, ornaments fell off the mantelpieces, babies woke and cried, there was no peace at all. “He does it out of badness, that’s what it is!” people said as another tremendous sneeze rocked the tea in their cups and made the bread and butter slide off the plates, "just out of badness, that's all."

At the end of a week the sneezing stopped. "The Giant's cold is better," they said to each other. No sound at all came from the Giant's valley. This was very odd. "Has he gone away?" they asked, "he's never been as quiet as this." "Perhaps he's sorry," someone suggested, but nobody really believed that. And in any case they had other things to think about. The new Town Hall was finished at last, the handsome building that had been rising slowly at the head of the street was completed, all but the weathercock which was to sit on the top of the little spire on the roof. The Mayor had invited the mayors and their ladies and the important people from towns and villages many miles round to come on Saturday for a celebration. What a day it was to be – bands, flags, fine clothes, dancing in the streets. No wonder they forgot about the Giant.

But they didn't forget about him for long because two things happened. Mr Clamber the steeplejack hurt his leg and had to stay in bed, and the builders of the Town Hall reported that the crane which was to hoist the handsome gilt weathercock to its proud place on the top of the spire had broken and there was no chance of repairing it in time. What could be done?

Nobody knew who it was who first whispered "The Giant could help!" Somebody whispered it and somebody else heard them and soon the whisper was so loud that everyone knew about it. "The Giant might help if he was asked. Someone will have to ask him!"

Who? Who could ask the Giant? The Mayor and two of his Aldermen went over into the Giant's valley on Friday evening, looking very serious and important. "He won't come," Tom said, "catch him coming! Catch him obliging anyone!"

But to the surprise of everyone the Mayor returned to say that the Giant had agreed to come that very evening. So the policeman moved the crowds to the side of the street and cleared away some of the parked cars so that the Giant could walk without his great boots knocking into them. "Here he comes!" the onlookers said, and at last there was the Giant himself, huge and slow, and a little shy because people were very glad to see him.

He picked up the weathercock between his finger and thumb.

"Nice bit of work here," he said. They explained to him how it was to be bolted into its place at the top of the spire. They handed him the nuts which looked like grains of sand in his enormous palm.

"No good," the Giant said, "they're too small, and my fingers are too big. I couldn't work with those, not if I tried for a year I couldn't." Then his eyes travelled over the crowd and lit on Tom. "But this young fellow could," he said, "he has the right size of hands for the job." And before he knew just what was happening Tom had the nuts thrust into one hand and a spanner placed in the other, he felt the great finger and thumb of the Giant nip him round his middle, and up he rose into the sky!

How odd it was up there, high above the roofs, with all those pink faces staring at him from under his feet and the Giant's warm hand tight round him! With his other hand the Giant had placed the golden bird in position. "Now young fellow!" the Giant said as he swung Tom over beside the weathercock. In no time at all Tom's hands had put the nuts on and tightened them.

What was that curious noise coming up from the sea of pink

faces? Cheering, that was what it was, they were cheering! The cheers grew louder and louder still as the Giant lowered Tom and set him on the ground again. How splendid the weathercock looked up there in the evening sky with the last of the evening sunlight brightening its feathers. What a grand day they would have tomorrow, after all. What a good-hearted fellow the Giant was, how clever Tom had been.

"Did you hear that?" teased the wind in Tom's ear, "cheering for you! For you and the Giant!" but the cheering was so loud that Tom took no notice at all.

A Leaf in the Shape of a Key

Joan Aiken

Leaves were falling from the trees, because it was the second day of November. It was also the day after Tim's birthday, and he had a new tricycle to ride in the garden.

First he fed the snails, who lived by the garden pond, with some orange jelly left over from his birthday tea. The snails loved orange jelly, and ate up a whole plateful. Tim would also have given some jelly to the stone goblin who sat by the garden pond, but the goblin was not fond of jelly. In fact, he never ate anything at all. He always looked gloomy and bad-tempered. Perhaps this was because one of his feet was stuck underneath a huge rock.

"Would you like to ride on my tricycle?" Tim suggested.

The goblin's eyes flashed. He looked as if he would like a ride very much.

But that was no good either, because Tim couldn't lift the rock, which was very heavy indeed.

Tim went off, riding his tricycle over the grass. The stone goblin stared after him.

Leaves were fluttering down all over the lawn, and because there had been a frost the night before the grass was all crunchy with white frost crystals.

As Tim pedalled about, he began catching the leaves when they floated near him, and putting them in the basket of his tricycle. He caught a red leaf, a yellow leaf, a brown leaf, a pale green leaf, a dark green leaf, and a silvery leaf. Then he caught another red leaf, two more brown leaves and two more yellow leaves. Then he caught a great green leaf, the shape of a hand. Presently his basket was almost filled up with leaves. He pedalled back to the pond and showed all his leaves to the snails and the stone goblin.

"Look! I have caught twelve leaves!"

Now the goblin began to pay attention. "If you have caught twelve leaves, all different," he said, "that's magic."

Tim spread his leaves on the grass and the goblin counted them.

"That one is a walnut leaf. And that's an oak leaf. This is a maple leaf. And that is from a silver birch. This one is from an apple tree. And that is a copper beech leaf. And here we have an ash leaf. And you also have a cob-nut leaf, a pear tree leaf, a rose leaf, a mulberry leaf and a fig leaf. You are a very lucky boy, Tim. You have caught twelve leaves, and all of them are different."

"What must I do now?" said Tim, very excited.

"You must catch one more leaf. And that will give you what you want most in the whole world."

On his birthday the day before Tim had been given his tricycle, and a lot of other presents, and he felt he already had most of the things he wanted.

But there *was* one other thing.

"Oh!" he said. "What I would *really* like is to be able to get into the little cave up above the garden pond."

There was a steep back on one side of the garden pond – almost like a little cliff – where water came trickling out of a hole and ran down into the pond.

In the cliff there was a tiny cave. It was no bigger than the inside of a teapot. You could see into it, and it was very beautiful, all lined with moss like green velvet. There were tiny flowers growing in the moss, no bigger than pin-heads. They were blue and white. Tim longed to be small enough to get inside this beautiful place.

The stone goblin's eyes flashed again.

"Ride off on your tricycle," he

said, "and catch one more leaf. Then bring it here. You must bring me the very first leaf that you catch."

Tim rode off at top speed. Almost at once a leaf came fluttering down in front of him and fell right into his basket.

"Watch out!" shouted a blackbird, swooping past him, very low. "Don't trust that goblin! He means mischief! I can see it in his eye."

But Tim took no notice of the blackbird's warning. He pedalled quickly back to the goblin with the thirteenth leaf in his basket.

"Here it is," he said, and he took it out.

The thirteenth leaf was pale brown, and it was in the shape of a key.

"Look in the middle of my stomach," said the goblin, "and you'll find a keyhole."

Tim looked, and he found the keyhole.

"Put in the key and turn it," said the goblin.

Tim put the key into the hole and turned it. He had a hard job, for it was very stiff, but it did turn.

As soon as Tim had turned the key, the goblin began to grow bigger. He pulled his foot out from under the heavy rock. He stood up, rather stiffly.

"That's better!" he said.

He was still growing, bigger and bigger.

"You promised that I should get into the cave," said Tim.

"So you shall," said the goblin.

He picked Tim up easily in his hand, reached over the pond, and put him into the cave.

"Why!" exclaimed Tim. "*You* weren't growing bigger. *I* was growing smaller!"

He was tremendously happy to be in the cave, and he began to clamber about, looking at the beautiful flowers. Now they seemed as big as teacups. But Tim found that, since *he* was so small, he sank up to his knees in the thick wet green moss, which was not very comfortable. Still, he was so pleased to be there that for some time he did not look out through the doorway, till he heard the blackbird squawking again.

When Tim did look out, he had quite a shock. For the stone goblin had climbed on to his tricycle and was pedalling away.

"Well, I did offer him a ride before," thought Tim.

But then he saw that the goblin was pedalling towards the garden gate, which opened into the road.

"Stop, stop!" shouted Tim. "I'm not allowed to go out there!

It's dangerous!"

But Tim had grown so small that his voice came out only as a tiny squeak. The goblin may not have heard. He took no notice at all. He was waving his arms about, singing and shouting, and pedalling crazily from side to side.

"I'm free!" he was shouting. "At last I'm free! I can go anywhere I want! I can go all over the world!"

Then Tim found out a frightening thing. He was so small that the little cliff under the cave entrance seemed terribly high to him, and there was no way down it. He was stuck in the cave.

"Help!" he shouted to the goblin.

"I can't climb down! Please come back and lift me down!"

"*I'm* not going to help you!" the goblin shouted back. "You should have thought of that before. You'll just have to stay there! Goodbye! You'll never seen me again."

And he pedalled right out of the garden gate.

Poor Tim stared down the terribly steep cliff at the pond below. The pond was like a huge lake. "Whatever shall I do?" he wondered. "Mum and Dad will never find me here. They'll never think of looking. I'm smaller than a mouse. I can't shout loud enough for them to hear me. I shall have to stay in this cave for ever and ever. What shall I eat?"

He sat down miserably on the wet green moss.

But he had not been sitting there very long when, to his surprise, he saw four long horns with eyes at their tips come poking up over the sill of the doorway. The horns belonged to two snails who had come climbing up the cliff. Snails don't mind how steep a cliff is, because they can stick themselves to the rock with their own glue.

"Don't worry now, Tim," they said kindly. "Just you hold on to us. We'll soon get you down the cliff. Hold tight on to our shells."

They turned themselves round. Tim put an arm round each of their shells, and they went slowly down the cliff, head first. It was a bit frightening for Tim, because they crawled so very slowly; he had rather too much time to look down. In the end he found it was better to look at the snails' shells, covered with beautiful pink and brown and yellow patterns, or to watch the clever way they stretched out their long necks and then pulled in their strong tails.

At last they came to the bottom of the cliff, and then, very carefully, they crawled round the stone edge of the pond, until Tim

was safely back on the grass again, beside the empty plate, which seemed as big as a whole room.

"Oh, thank you!" said Tim. "I thought I would *never* get out of there! It was very kind of you."

"It was nothing," said the snails politely. "After all, you gave us all that orange jelly."

Tim was safely out of the cave. But he was still tiny, much smaller than a mouse, and he didn't know what to do about that.

And the stone goblin had gone off with his tricycle.

But just at the moment he heard a tremendous crash in the road beyond the hedge.

And at that very same moment, Tim grew back to his right size again.

Five minutes later, Tim's father came into the garden, looking both angry and puzzled. He was carrying Tim's tricycle.

"Tim! How did this get into the road?" he said. "I found it up by the crossroads. The front wheel is bent – some car must have run into it. And there are bits of broken stone all over the street. Have you been riding out there? You know you are not allowed to do that."

"The stone goblin took it," said Tim.

"Don't talk nonsense!"

"But look! He's gone!"

Tim's father looked at the empty place where the goblin had been, and at the heavy rock. It was much too heavy for Tim to have lifted. So was the goblin.

Tim's father scratched his head. Then he fetched his tools and straightened out the front wheel.

"No riding in the street, now!" he said.

"Of course not," said Tim.

He began riding over the grass again. He caught lots more falling leaves. But he never again caught twelve different kinds.

The stone goblin never came back.

But whenever there was orange jelly for tea, Tim remembered to give some to the snails.

The Korean Cinderella

Shirley Climo

Long ago in Korea, when magical creatures were as common as cabbages, there lived an old gentleman and his wife. For years they longed for a child to share their tile-roofed cottage. At last a daughter was born.

"Good fortune!" the old man exclaimed. "I'll plant a pear tree in the courtyard to celebrate this day!"

"And Pear Blossom will be our daughter's name," the old woman added.

Both the tree and the child grew lovelier with each passing season. In spring white flowers frosted the tree, and Pear Blossom wore a white ribbon on her long, black braid. In summer, when the tree bent with ripening fruit, Pear Blossom's mother wove a band of rosy gold into her hair. In the autumn, when leaves from the tree blew about the courtyard like scraps of sunshine, her mother dressed Pear Blossom in a yellow gown. But one winter day, when the branches on the pear tree were still bare sticks, the old woman died.

"*Aigo*!" wailed the old man. "Who will tend Pear Blossom now?"

He put on his tall horsehair hat and went to the village matchmaker. She knew of a widow with a daughter. The girl, named Peony, was just the age of Pear Blossom.

"Three in one!" promised the matchmaker. "A wife for you and a mother and a sister for Pear Blossom."

So the old gentleman took the widow for his wife. Although Pear Blossom called the woman *Omoni*, or Mother, she was far from motherly. And Peony was worse than no sister at all.

Omoni found fault as soon as she stepped into the kitchen. "Too cold!" she grumbled. "The fire's gone out. Fetch wood, Pear Blossom. Be quick!"

Pear Blossom gathered sticks and fed the stove until the lid on the kettle danced from steam.

"Too hot!" her stepmother scolded then. "The noodles are scorching. Get water, Pear Blossom. Be quick!"

Both Omoni and Peony were jealous of Pear Blossom, and the harder she worked the happier they were. Each day Pear Blossom was up before the *Hai*, the sun. She cooked and cleaned until midnight, with only the crickets for company.

Each year was worse than the one before, for her father grew too feeble to pay attention to Pear Blossom's troubles.

Omoni dressed Pear Blossom in rags and tied her shiny braid with a twist of rope. And now she and Peony addressed her only as Little Pig or Pigling.

"Pigling has a pigtail!" jeered Peony.

But nothing could hide Pear Blossom's beauty. At night Omoni lay sleepless, searching for an excuse to get rid of her stepdaughter. One morning she told Pear Blossom, "The water jar by the door needs filling."

"It leaks, Omoni," Pear Blossom replied, "for it has a hole the size of an onion."

"Stubborn little pigs get tied up and taken to market!" warned her stepmother. "Fill that jar!"

Then Omoni and Peony marched through the courtyard gate, locking it behind them.

Pear Blossom leaned against the tall jar. "Will none in this world help me?" she asked.

"Jug-jug-jugful!" rumbled a

hoarse voice.

"A *tokgabi*!" Pear Blossom gasped. "A goblin!" What if a tokgabi goblin were hiding in the jar? Fearfully, she stood on tiptoe and peered inside.

A gigantic frog with bulging eyes stared back. "Jugful!" it croaked again, and squeezed itself like a stopper into the hole in the jar.

"As you wish," agreed Pear Blossom, for, frog or goblin, it was best to do its bidding. She hurried to the well and drew a jugful of water. When she poured it into the jar, not a drop leaked out!

When Omoni and Peony returned, they found Pear Blossom

resting beside the jar. "So!" Omoni shrilled. "Off to market, Little Pig!"

"But Omoni, the jar is full," Pear Blossom protested. "A frog helped me."

"Trickery!" snapped her stepmother, but she muttered to Peony, "A magic frog! Look inside that jar!"

Peony hung over the rim but saw only her own scowling face. All of a sudden the jar tipped. A flood of water soaked Peony from head to toes. "Pigling's to blame!" she howled.

"Someday Little Pig will get what she deserves!" Omoni

declared. She made Pear Blossom crawl through the puddles, licking up the water.

The next morning Omoni scattered a huge sack of rice around the courtyard. “Hull this rice, Little Pig,” she ordered. “Polish every grain. Or else” – she shook the empty bag – “YOU’LL be put in this sack and sent to China.”

Then Omoni and Peony left for the village.

Rice covered the ground like sand beside the sea. Pear Blossom threw her arms around the pear tree and asked, “Will none in this world help me?”

Wings whirred overhead, and a flock of sparrows flew out of the tree. "Cheer! Cheer! Cheer!" the sparrows called to Pear Blossom. They pecked at the rice, separating husk from kernel. In a matter of minutes the sparrows had polished the rice and piled it in a corner.

When Omoni came back, she found Pear Blossom nodding beneath the tree. "Off to China!" her stepmother began, and then caught sight of the mound of rice. "How can this be?" she demanded.

Pear Blossom rubbed her eyes. "Sparrows flew out of the tree and polished the rice."

"Birds don't hull rice," scoffed

Omoni. "They *eat* it!" But to Peony she whispered, "It's magic that's flying about! Catch some!" She pushed Peony beneath the tree.

At once the cloud of sparrows swooped down. "Cheat! Cheat! Cheat!" they chattered at Peony. They pecked at her, tearing her jacket. They perched on her head, pulling her hair.

"Pigling's to blame!" Peony bawled.

"Someday Little Pig will get what she deserves!" Omoni threatened. She did not give Pear Blossom anything to eat, not that day or the next, not so much as a kernel of rice.

Pear Blossom had food to fix nevertheless. The village was having a festival, and she had to pack picnic hampers of dried fish and pickled cabbage for her stepmother. She also sewed a dress of pink silk for her stepsister. When festival day came, Peony mocked Pear Blossom, calling her "Dirty-Piglet-Stay-at-Home."

"Pigling may go," said Omoni in a voice as sweet as barley sugar, "after she weeds the rice paddies." She handed Pear Blossom a basket of wilted turnip tops. "Here is Pigling's picnic."

"I am most grateful, Honourable Mother," said Pear Blossom.

When she reached the fields, Pear Blossom dropped the basket in dismay. Rice rippled before her like a great, green lake. Weeding it would take weeks. "Who could do such a task?" she asked.

Suddenly a whirlwind twisted through the fields, and a huge black ox reared up from a cloud of dust. "DO-O-O!" it bellowed, tossing its great horns.

The ox began to munch the weeds, moving through the rows of rice faster than the wind itself. Each mouthful brought it closer to Pear Blossom. Even though she hid her face in her hands, she heard the crunch of its teeth and felt the beast's warm breath on her neck.

At last she dared to peek between her fingers. Both ox and weeds were gone. Hoofprints big as cartwheels pocked the field, yet not a single blade of rice was trampled. And when Pear Blossom looked in her basket, she found fruit and honey candy instead of turnips!

She bowed, then cupped her hands and called, "A thousand thanks!"

Pear Blossom hastened to the village festival. The road, which followed a crooked stream, was rough with pebbles. Pear Blossom had just slipped off one straw sandal to shake out a stone when she heard a shout.

"Make way! Make way for the magistrate!"

Four bearers, a palanquin swaying on poles across their shoulders, jogged toward her. In the chair sat a young nobleman dressed in rich robes and wearing a jade jewel in his topknot. Flustered, Pear Blossom teetered on one leg like a crane, holding her straw sandal. Her cheeks grew hot as red peppers, and she hopped behind a willow tree that grew beside the stream. As she did, her sandal splashed into the water and bobbed like a small boat, just out of reach.

"Stop!" commanded the magistrate from his palanquin.

He was calling to his bearers. But Pear Blossom thought he was shouting at her, and, frightened, she fled down the road.

The magistrate gazed after Pear Blossom, struck by her beauty. Then he ordered his men to fish her sandal from the stream and to carry him back to the village.

At the festival Pear Blossom forgot about her missing shoe. She watched the acrobats and tightrope walkers until she was dizzy. She listened to the flutes and drums until her ears rang. She nibbled on treats until her basket was almost empty.

She was peeling the last orange when Omoni and Peony came upon her.

"Little Pig!" screamed her

stepmother. "What are you doing here?"

"I am here because a great black ox ate all the weeds in the rice paddies," said Pear Blossom. "The same ox that gave me this orange."

"Black ox indeed!" Omoni snorted. "Oxen are brown. You stole that fruit—" She was interrupted by the magistrate's bearers.

"Hear this!" they shouted as they elbowed the palanquin through the crowd. "We seek the girl with one shoe!"

"It's Pigling!" Peony pointed at her sister. "She's lost her shoe."

The bearers put the chair down

beside Pear Blossom, and the nobleman held up the straw sandal.

"The magistrate has come to arrest you for stealing!" Omoni shook Pear Blossom. "NOW you'll get what you deserve!"

"Then she must deserve *me* as her husband," said the magistrate, "for this lucky shoe has led me to her."

"Another of Pigling's magic tricks!" hissed Omoni, pulling Peony to the palanquin. "*My* daughter will give you TWO shoes! That is twice as lucky!"

The magistrate looked at Omoni as if she had lost her wits; then he turned to Pear Blossom and said, “I’ve luck enough if she who wears *this* one becomes my bride.”

Pear Blossom smiled, too shy to speak, and slipped the sandal on her foot.

Omoni stood staring, stiff as a clay statue, but Peony ran straight

to the rice fields to find the magic ox. All she saw was a glimpse of its hooves as it galloped away.

When springtime came, the magistrate sent a go-between to Pear Blossom's old father to arrange a grand marriage. Pear Blossom's wedding slippers were of silk, and in the courtyard of her splendid new house, a dozen pear trees bloomed. "Ewha! Ewha!" chirruped the sparrows in the branches. "E-WHA!" croaked the giant frog down below.

That is as it was long ago, and as it should be. For, in Korea, *Ewha* means "Pear Blossom".

The King Who Wanted to Touch the Moon

Margaret Mayo

Long ago there lived a king who always had to have his own way. Everyone had to do exactly what he said. Immediately. No talk, no arguing.

Well, one night this king looked out of the window and saw the silvery moon riding high in the sky and, there and then, he wanted to reach out and touch it. But even he couldn't do that. So he thought about it, and he thought about it. Night and day he thought about it. And at last he worked out a way of touching the moon. He would have a tall, tall tower built that reached to the sky, and then, when he had climbed to the top, he would be able to touch the moon.

So the king sent for the royal carpenter and ordered him to build the tower.

The carpenter shook his head. "A tower so tall that it reaches right to the moon? Your majesty, it is not possible. It can't be done."

"Can't!" shouted the king. "No

such word as can't in this kingdom. Come back tomorrow morning, first thing, and tell me exactly how you are going to build my tower."

That night the carpenter did some hard thinking, and in the end he worked out a way of building a tall tower.

The next morning he went to the king and said, "Your majesty, the way to build the tower is to pile up lots of strong wooden chests, one on top of the other, hundreds and thousands of them, until they reach to the sky."

Now the king liked this idea. So he ordered his subjects to search their homes and bring all their strong chests to the palace. Immediately. And if anyone refused? Well, there was plenty of room in the royal prisons for them.

So, of course, the people brought their chests and gave them to the king. And there were all kinds of chests – big and small, carved, polished, painted and plain.

Then the carpenter and his assistant set to work. They laid chest upon chest, one on top of the other, up and up, and before long, outside the palace, there stood a tall tower. But when all the chests had been used, the tower did not even reach to the clouds.

The king said to the carpenter, "Make some more chests!"

So wood was found and the carpenter and his assistant sawed and hammered and made more chests. Then they added these to the tower, laying chest upon chest, one on top of the other, up and up. But when all the chests had been used, the tower only reached to the clouds.

The king said to the carpenter, "Make some more chests!"

"There is no more wood, your majesty," said the carpenter.

"Then cut down all the trees and get some wood," ordered the king.

The carpenter shook his head. "*All* the trees!" he said. "Oh no, we can't do that—"

"Did I hear you say 'can't'? Have you forgotten that there is no such word as 'can't' in this kingdom?" said the king. "Go and cut down *all* the trees. Immediately."

So then all the trees in the kingdom were chopped down – the great ancient trees and the slender saplings, the fruit trees and the nut trees and the flowering trees – all were cut down and sawn into planks and made into chests. More and more chests. And the chests were laid one on top of the other. Up and up. And when all the chests had been used, the tower reached beyond the clouds and up into the sky.

The king looked at the tower and he was pleased. He said, "The time has come for me to climb my tall, tall tower and touch the moon."

He began to climb, up and up and up, until at last he stood at the top of his tall, tall tower. He looked up and he stretched out both his arms, but he could not quite reach to the moon. He stood on the very tips of his toes and stretched some more. He was so close. He could almost touch the moon. But not quite.

He shouted down. "Bring up

another chest! Just one! That will be enough!"

The carpenter looked around. There were no chests left. No wood left. And not a single tree in all the land.

So he called out, "Your majesty, there are *no more chests*!"

The king shouted back, "THEN TAKE ONE OUT FROM THE BOTTOM AND BRING THAT UP HERE."

The carpenter was astonished. He couldn't take a chest out from the bottom of the pile. Well, could he? Surely, the king was not serious. Then he heard the king shouting again.

"DIDN'T YOU HEAR ME? TAKE ONE OUT FROM THE BOTTOM! IMMEDIATELY!"

The carpenter raised his eyebrows, shrugged his shoulders and then did as he was told. He pulled a chest out from the bottom of the pile.

And you can imagine what happened next. The whole tall tower came tumbling down, king, chests and all. So that was the end of the king who always had to have his own way and who wanted, above everything else, to touch the moon.

Mr Pepperpot Buys Macaroni

Alf Prøysen

"It's a very long time since we've had macaroni for supper," said Mr Pepperpot one day.

"Then you shall have it today, my love," said his wife. "But I shall have to go to the grocer for some. So first of all you'll have to find me."

"Find you?" said Mr Pepperpot. "What sort of nonsense is that?" But when he looked round for her he couldn't see her anywhere. "Don't be silly, wife," he said, "if you're hiding in the cupboard you must come out this minute. We're too big to play hide-and-seek."

"*I'm* not too big, I'm just the right size for 'hunt-the-pepperpot'," laughed Mrs Pepperpot. "Find me if you can!"

"I'm not going to charge round my own bedroom looking for my wife," he said crossly.

"Now, now! I'll help you; I'll tell you when you're warm. Just now you're very cold." For Mr

Pepperpot was peering out of the window, thinking she might have jumped out. As he searched round the room she called out. "Warm!", "Colder!", "Getting hotter!" until he was quite dizzy.

At last she shouted, "You'll burn the top of your bald head if you don't look up!" And there she was, sitting on the bedpost, swinging her legs and laughing at him.

Her husband pulled a very long face when he saw her. "This is a bad business – a very bad business," he said, stroking her cheek with his little finger.

"I don't think it's a bad business," said Mrs Pepperpot.

"I shall have a terrible time. The whole town will laugh when they see I have a wife the size of a pepperpot."

"Who cares?" she answered. "That doesn't matter a bit. Now put me down on the floor so that I can get ready to go to the grocer and buy your macaroni."

But her husband wouldn't hear of her going; he would go to the grocer himself.

"That'll be a lot of use!" she said. "When you get home you'll have forgotten to buy the macaroni. I'm sure even if I wrote 'macaroni' right across your forehead you'd bring back cinnamon and salt herrings instead."

"But how are you going to walk all that way with those tiny legs?"

"Put me in your coat pocket; then I won't need to walk."

There was no help for it, so Mr Pepperpot put his wife in his pocket and set off for the shop.

Soon she started talking, "My goodness me, what a lot of strange things you have in your pocket – screws and nails, tobacco and matches – there's even a fishhook! You'll have to take that out at once; I might get it caught in my skirt."

"Don't talk so loud," said her husband as he took out the fish-hook. "We're going into the shop now."

It was an old-fashioned village store where they sold everything from prunes to coffee cups. The grocer was particularly proud of the coffee cups and held one up for Mr Pepperpot to see. This made his wife curious and she popped her head out of his pocket.

"You stay where you are!" whispered Mr Pepperpot.

"I beg your pardon, did you say anything?" asked the grocer.

"No, no, I was just humming a little tune," said Mr Pepperpot. "Tra-la-la!"

"What colour are the cups?" whispered his wife. And her husband sang:

"The cups are blue
With gold edge too,
But they cost too much
So that won't do!"

After that Mrs Pepperpot kept

quiet – but not for long. When her husband pulled out his tobacco tin she couldn't resist hanging on to the lid. Neither her husband nor anyone else in the shop noticed her slipping on to the counter and hiding behind a flour-bag. From there she darted silently across to the scales, crawled under them, past a pair of kippers wrapped in newspaper, and found herself next to the coffee cups.

"Aren't they pretty!" she whispered, and took a step backwards to get a better view. Whoops! She fell right into the macaroni drawer which had been left open. She hastily covered herself up with macaroni, but the grocer heard the scratching noise and quickly banged the drawer shut. You see, it did sometimes happen that mice got in the drawers, and that's not the sort of thing you want people to know about, so the grocer pretended nothing had happened and went on serving.

There was Mrs Pepperpot all in the dark; she could hear the grocer serving her husband now. "That's good," she thought. "When he orders macaroni I'll get my chance to slip into the bag with it."

But it was just as she had feared;

her husband forgot what he had come to buy. Mrs Pepperpot shouted at the top of her voice, "MACARONI!", but it was impossible to get him to hear.

"A quarter of a pound of coffee, please," said her husband.

"Anything else?" asked the grocer.

"MACARONI!" shouted Mrs Pepperpot.

"Two pounds of sugar," said her husband.

"Anything more?"

"MACARONI!" shouted Mrs Pepperpot.

But at last her husband remembered the macaroni of his own accord. The grocer hurriedly filled a bag. He thought he felt something move, but he didn't say a word.

"That's all, thank you," said Mr Pepperpot. When he got outside the door he was just about to make sure his wife was still in his pocket when a van drew up and offered to give him a lift all the way home. Once there he took off his knapsack with all the shopping in it and put his hand in his pocket to lift out his wife.

The pocket was empty.

Now he was really frightened. First he thought she was teasing him, but when he had called three times and still no wife appeared, he put on his hat again and hurried back to the shop.

The grocer saw him coming. "He's probably going to complain about the mouse in the macaroni," he thought.

"Have you forgotten something, Mr Pepperpot?" he asked, and

smiled as pleasantly as he could.

Mr Pepperpot was looking all round. “Yes,” he said.

“I would be very grateful, Mr Pepperpot, if you would keep it to yourself about the mouse being in the macaroni. I’ll let you have these fine blue coffee cups if you’ll say no more about it.”

“Mouse?” Mr Pepperpot looked puzzled.

“Shh!” said the grocer, and hurriedly started wrapping up the cups.

Then Mr Pepperpot realised that the grocer had mistaken his wife for a mouse. So he took the cups and rushed home as fast as he could. By the time he got there he was in a sweat of fear that his wife might have been squeezed to death in the macaroni bag.

"Oh, my dear wife," he muttered to himself. "My poor darling wife. I'll never again be ashamed of you being the size of a pepperpot – as long as you're still alive!"

When he opened the door she was standing by the cooking-stove, dishing up the macaroni – as large as life; in fact, as large as you or I.

Ticky Picky Boom Boom

Pat Thomson

Stories about Ananse the trickster spider are well-known in both Africa and the West Indies. This story is from Jamaica. It is about Ananse's longing for a flower garden and how Mr Tiger dug the bed for his plants.

Ananse the trickster had a very fine vegetable garden. He had every vegetable imaginable; plenty of potatoes and more yams than he could eat. But there was one thing he did not have: a flower garden, and Ananse wanted above all to have flowers, just like a rich man.

"I shall turn the yam patch into a flower garden," he decided, "and I shall make Mr Tiger dig the flower bed for me."

Now Mr Tiger had been tricked by Ananse before and he was cautious.

"What will you give me if I dig

out the yams?" he asked.

"You may keep all the yams you dig up," replied Ananse.

Mr Tiger was satisfied with that. He loved to eat yams. So, early next morning, he began to dig Ananse's garden for him. All day, he dug and dug, but the harder he worked, the deeper the yams seemed to sink into the ground. By the end of the day, Ananse's garden was thoroughly turned over, but Mr Tiger had not been able to get any yams for himself at all.

Mr Tiger was hot, tired and furious. This was another of Ananse's tricks! He lost his temper and chopped at one of the yams. He chopped it into little pieces, and then set off for home, muttering angrily.

What was that?

Behind him, Mr Tiger heard a noise. A shuffling noise at first and then a stamping of small feet. Mr Tiger turned around – and along the road behind him, walking on little vegetable legs, came the yams! The noise that their feet made went like this:

Ticky picky boom boom
Ticky picky boom boom
Ticky picky boom boom bouf!

Tiger began to run.

The yams began to run, too.

Tiger began to gallop.

The yams began to gallop.

Tiger jumped.

The yams jumped.

Mr Tiger made straight for Mr Dog's house, running as fast as he could.

"Brother Dog," he shouted, "hide

me! The yams are coming."

"All right," said Brother Dog. "Hide behind me but don't say a word."

So Mr Tiger hid behind Dog.

And down the road came the yams and the noise that their feet made sounded like this:

Ticky picky boom boom
Ticky picky boom boom
Ticky picky boom boom bouf!

The yams said, "Brother Dog, have you seen Mr Tiger?"

And Brother Dog looked straight ahead and said, "I can't see Mr Tiger anywhere, not at all."

But Mr Tiger was so frightened

that he called out, "Don't tell them, Brother Dog!" and Dog was so cross that he ran off and left Mr Tiger to the yams.

And the yams jumped.

And Tiger jumped.

And the yams ran.

And Tiger ran.

And the yams galloped.

And Tiger galloped.

Then Mr Tiger saw Sister Duck and all her little ducklings, so he hurried up to her and said, "Sister Duck, hide me! The yams are coming!"

"All right," said Sister Duck. "Get behind me but don't say a word."

So Mr Tiger hid behind Sister Duck.

And down the road came the yams, and the noise that their feet made sounded like this:

Ticky picky boom boom
Ticky picky boom boom
Ticky picky boom boom bouf!

The yams said, "Sister Duck, have you seen Mr Tiger?"

And Sister Duck looked straight ahead and said, "Well now, I can't see him anywhere. Nowhere at all."

But Mr Tiger was so frightened he shouted out, "Don't tell them, Sister Duck," and Sister Duck was so cross that she moved away and left him to the yams.

And the yams jumped.

And Tiger jumped.

And the yams ran.

And Tiger ran.

And the yams galloped.

And Tiger galloped.

He galloped and galloped, but he was getting tired, and still he could hear the yams coming along the road behind him, getting nearer and nearer. At last, he came to a stream and over the stream was a little plank bridge. On the other side was Mr Goat.

Mr Tiger ran across the bridge and called out, "Mr Goat, hide me! The yams are coming!"

"All right," said Mr Goat, "but don't say a word."

So Mr Tiger hid behind Mr Goat.

And down the road came the yams, and the noise that their feet made sounded like this:

Ticky picky boom boom
Ticky picky boom boom
Ticky picky boom boom bouf!

When they reached the bridge, they called out, "Mr Goat, have you seen Mr Tiger?"

And Mr Goat looked straight ahead but before he could say anything, Mr Tiger shouted, "Don't tell them, Mr Goat, don't tell them."

The yams jumped on to the bridge but so did Mr Goat, and he just put down his head and butted them into the stream. Then Mr Goat and Mr Tiger picked the pieces out of the water and took them home to make a great feast of yams. But they certainly did *not* invite Ananse to the feast.

When the nights are dark, Mr Tiger stays at home. He dare not walk along the road, for behind him, he still thinks he hears a noise which sounds like this:

Ticky picky boom boom
Ticky picky boom boom
Ticky picky boom boom bouf!

ACKNOWLEDGEMENTS

The publishers wish to thank the following for permission to reproduce copyright material:

Pat Thomson: "Ticky Picky Boom Boom" included in *A Pocketful of Stories for Five Year Olds*; Copyright 1991 Pat Thomson; first published by Doubleday; reproduced by permission of Laura Cecil Literary Agency.

Alison Uttley: "Sam Pig Seeks His Fortune" from *Sam Pig Seeks His Fortune* by Alison Uttley; reproduced by permission of Faber and Faber Ltd.

Ruth Ainsworth: "The Mermaid's Crown"; reproduced by permission of R. F. Gilbert.

David L. Harrison: "The Giant Who Threw Tantrums" from *The Book of Giant Stories* by David L. Harrison; first published by Jonathan Cape 1972 and reproduced with their permission.

Joan Aiken: "A Leaf in the Shape of a Key" from *The Last Slice of Rainbow* by Joan Aiken; Copyright Joan Aiken Enterprises Ltd; first published by Jonathan Cape 1985 and reproduced by permission of A. M. Heath & Co Ltd on behalf of the author.

Andrew Matthews: "The Cow Who Flew" from *The Beasts of Boggart Hollow* by Andrew Matthews; first published by Orion Children's Books 1996 and reproduced with their permission.

Margaret Mahy: "The Boy with Two Shadows" from *A Lion in the Meadows and Five Other Favourites* by Margaret Mahy; first published by Orion Children's Books 1976 and reproduced with their permission.

Anon: "The Magic Broom" (original title "Phillipippa") from *My Holiday Book*, ed. Mrs Herbert Strang; first published by Oxford University Press 1936 and reproduced with their permission.

Linda Allen: *Mrs Simkin and the Magic Wheelbarrow*. Copyright Linda Allen 1987; first published by Hamish Hamilton 1987 and reproduced by permission of Penguin Books Ltd.

Alf Prøysen: "Mr Pepperpot Buys Macaroni" from *Mrs Pepperpot and the Macaroni*, first published by Red Fox 1992, pp. 24–31, and an extract reproduced by permission of Random House UK.

ACKNOWLEDGEMENTS

Heather Eyles: "Tim's Tooth" from *The Much Better Story Book*; first published by Red Fox 1992, pp. 109–16, and reproduced by permission of Westminster Children's Hospital School.

Janet McNeill: "The Gigantic Baldness" included in *Bad Boys*, compiled by Eileen Colwell; first published by Puffin 1972; reproduced by permission of A. P. Watt Ltd on behalf of the author.

Margaret Mayo: "The King Who Wanted to Touch the Moon" from *The Orchard Book of Magical Stories* by Margaret Mayo; first published by Orchard Books 1993, pp. 54–8 and reproduced by permission of The Watts Publishing Group Ltd.

Shirley Climo: *The Korean Cinderella* copyright © 1993 Shirley Climo, reproduced by permission of HarperCollins Publishers.

Every effort has been made to trace the copyright holders but where this has not been possible or where any error has been made the publishers will be pleased to make the necessary arrangement at the first opportunity.